M'TOTO

THE ADVENTURES OF
A BABY ELEPHANT

THE ADVENTURES OF

McGRAW-HILL BOOK COMPANY

M'TOTO

A BABY ELEPHANT

by Alyce Shinn Fechter

illustrated by Bernard Garbutt

New York   Toronto   London

Contents

CHAPTER ONE

M'*Toto's First Day*

The quiet hum and rustle of the life that teems in the green forests and yellowing prairies or veldts of East Africa were shocked into stunned silence. Shrieks and trumpet calls of joy echoed over and over in waves of homage.

"O O O M pah! O O o m pah!" trumpeted the Queen of the elephants.

"O O O M P A H! O O o o m pah!" trumpeted the elephant aunties that stood by the Queen.

"O O O O M M P A H!" they all trumpeted together. "*The Prince is Born!*"

"B R A A A V O O O!" answered the great King elephant, lifting his nine-foot tusks high into the air. The cheering trumpet calls sounded throughout the herd of eighty elephants standing under the huge trees in the African forest.

M'Toto, the baby elephant, had just been born. He rested in a kneeling position with his trunk curled under his head as the happy cheers swirled around him. He felt a gentle rubbing all over his furry little body and sighed contentedly.

A strong gentle trunk moved under him and lifted him a little way into the air and then lowered him slowly.

M'Toto opened his eyes wide with surprise to find himself standing on four small stumpy legs. They quivered and wobbled and he swayed from side to side as he tried again to lie down.

The mother elephant held him up and pushed him forward. He struggled to keep his trembling little legs under him but they shook and wavered and the left rear one just—stuck! The auntie elephant pushed the tardy left leg up with the others and together the big elephants nudged and pushed and prodded as M'Toto took his first, unwilling steps.

The little elephant raised his head to look around. There seemed to be many big grey objects moving all around him but the Queen and auntie urged him on until he felt something damp on his forehead. There was a sweet smell that he wanted very much to taste. He opened his mouth and suckled his first milk as his mother caressed and softly blew against his small fuzzy body.

All at once there was a great clamor among the herd. M'Toto shook with fright. Loud trumpeting screams and bellows echoed through the forest. "Lions! Lions! They have scented our little ones!"

Before M'Toto could cry out his mother grabbed him up and raced with him out of the forest onto the big prairie.

The eighty elephants were making a deafening clamor and M'Toto folded his ears down tightly to his head to shut out the noise. He and his mother were quickly herded into the middle of the group with the young elephants. The great bull and female elephants who had long ivory tusks formed a circle around them and faced outward to the danger.

A majestic black-maned lion and his lioness stopped at the edge of the forest facing the threatening ring of elephants. They switched their tails angrily and roared back their defiance before turning and disappearing down a dry stream bed usually called a *lugga* in Africa.

The tall Queen, breathing heavily, lay down on her side. With her trunk still around M'Toto, she fed him but she was very tired after running with her 200-pound baby. Soon she closed her eyes to sleep.

M'Toto finished nursing and looked over her great body and felt around her head with his little trunk. She opened one eye and smiled at him. He promptly poked at her eye. Then he turned his little trunk around and looked in the end of it. He moved this strange appendage around and then looked at his mother with round questioning eyes.

"That is your 'trunk,' M'Toto. You can smell with it, call through it, draw water into it to spray on your back, and do many other wonderful things with it, but now rest quietly with me. I am very tired and must try to sleep." The Queen again closed her eyes and sighed.

But M'Toto wasn't sleepy; he studied the little trunk which was only about twelve inches long. Then using the two little fingers on its tip he grabbed his mother's eyelashes and tried to raise them up.

One of the auntie elephants reached over and pulled M'Toto to her side. "Let your mother rest, M'Toto! I am your Aunt Karia. I'll help take care of you until you are a big boy elephant."

The little elephant snuffled over her lowered head and trunk, enjoying the new sensation. He felt security in her gentle grasp but there was a difference he could not understand. He looked into the eyes of his auntie and his small fuzzy brow wrinkled up with wonder.

"You will soon learn that each of us has a different odor, little one." Aunt Karia lowered her head farther and lovingly rubbed it against the furry little elephant.

M'Toto promptly grabbed at her eye.

"Don't do that, M'Toto! An eye is not a plaything, it is to see with and it hurts very much when you poke at it." Aunt Karia quickly raised her head out of reach.

Just then M'Toto became aware of a new odor and the earth under his little round feet trembled slightly. The new smell was very close to him but he had heard nothing. He turned around as quickly as his wobbly little legs would allow and started looking up—and *up*—and UP! A great, tall elephant, with long long yellow and white tusks, stood right behind him.

The little elephant started to back up between Aunt Karia's front feet but she placed them together and pushed him out in front of the great beast.

"This is the 'King' elephant, M'Toto. He is your father; you must always obey him," the auntie said.

The huge elephant touched the little one gently on the head, lifting first one little round ear and then the other. He felt all over the little body and caressed each stumpy little leg. M'Toto stood very still and tried very hard not to quiver, but he was a little frightened by this tremendous King elephant.

11

When the King had finished his inspection he turned toward M'Toto's mother, who was now sitting up watching. The King touched her tenderly on the forehead and they clasped their trunks for a long moment.

As he turned to move off and lead the herd to another forest, he looked back at the mother with a proud smile. "He'll do, Queen, he'll do!"

And the gentle spring rains descended upon the African landscape, wetting the great, hot bodies of the elephants who cheered these great blessings with their trumpet calls and shrieks of joy.

CHAPTER TWO

M'*Toto Grows Mischievous*

M'Toto grew stronger each day, but the stronger M'Toto grew the more trouble he caused. He was *so* full of mischief.

He would drink his fill of the rich milk and then poke his mother with his sharp little "milk" tusks and squeal with anger when she punished him.

He liked to slip between the tall legs of the big elephants and run off with the younger members of the herd. The aunties or his mother would have to follow him and send him back to his place with a tweak of one of his round ears and a thump across his fat little bottom.

Worst of all, he refused to go near the pool. The Queen was quite troubled since all of the elephants she had known loved water.

"We *must* bathe, M'Toto!" She tried to explain. "Our skins get too dry without water," she said as she sprayed him with water. But M'Toto just squealed the louder and stomped his round little feet and thrashed at her with his small trunk.

"Come, let me show you how nice it can be." The Queen lifted the baby elephant and carried him out into the muddy pool.

He cried and wiggled as she set him down in water that came up to his neck. Instinctively he rolled his trunk up on top of his head so if he slipped under the water he could still breathe.

Patiently she showed him how to suck up water with his trunk and blow it out at her and this he soon enjoyed. When he grew tired she led him back to the bank to nap under the care of one of the aunties.

After several hours of soaking in the warm water the Queen awakened M'Toto and they ambled back with the herd into the forest to eat leaves and twigs. As the day grew hotter they returned to the pool to cool their bodies but again M'Toto refused to enter the water.

"Very well, M'Toto," sighed his mother. "You can stay here on the bank while I take my bath." But as soon as she turned her back he darted through the tall reeds that lined the edge of the lake which stretched for a great distance.

He stopped suddenly. There was something big in the water. It was watching him! He squealed with fright as it opened a mouth large enough for M'Toto to walk right into, then slowly the big head sank under the water and small bubbles rose up where it had disappeared.

M'Toto had backed quickly out of the thick water plants. Now he wondered. "Did *I* scare that great big—thing?" Full of curiousity he went quietly forward for a closer look.

Again the animal raised its head above the water.

It looked a long time at M'Toto and then opened its frightening mouth and let out a "Hoosh! Haw, Haw, Haw!" This sent M'Toto rocking back on his haunches. He trumpeted in terror and turned to run but just then his mother grabbed him and swung him around behind her.

"Kiboko! You ugly hippopotamus! What are you doing to my baby?"

Kiboko opened her ugly mouth. Six tremendous curved tusks, each of the lower ones some three feet long, gleamed in the afternoon sun. She slowly raised her pink and grey body out of the water. The water cascaded down the thick folds of her 6,000-pound body and her short legs wavered for a moment as she flicked her small ears rapidly at the Queen elephant and M'Toto. M'Toto peered cautiously around his mother's flank.

The Queen fanned her ears out straight, held her trunk stiffly in front of her and blew an angry blast at the hippopotamus. Then she curled it back under her chin as though she were about to charge.

Kiboko sank back down into the pool, causing many small waves as she mooed, "Well look after your youngster if you don't want him frightened! I only yawned at him!" Not waiting for a response, she slowly disappeared from sight under the water.

M'Toto clutched his mother's tail as she guided him back to their end of the water hole. This time she pushed him into the water and let him scream all he wanted to while she finished her bath.

"It is now time to return to the forest for lunch," M'Toto heard the King trumpet. The whole herd slowly left the pool and ambled good-naturedly back to the forest to eat and doze through the rest of the day.

As the big elephants finished eating they stood dozing

and calmly tossing dust over their bodies to keep away the flies. The rumble of their full stomachs and an occasional snore from one of the dozing animals bored the baby elephant. It was much too quiet and peaceful under the large spreading trees.

M'Toto wandered off. He just could *not* stay in one place for long. He had learned to put one rear foot down in the same place the front foot left. So his feet went in single file. The soft pads with five round toenails on each front foot and four round toenails on each hind foot made no sound at all in the soft earth.

He passed quietly through the tall timber into a bamboo grove. M'Toto was not big enough to eat bamboo but he would pull up the sprouts and taste them and then toss them to one side. There was so much that was new to the baby elephant.

He smelled the ground eagerly with his little trunk, then thrust it up into the air as he sampled all the interesting smells that came to him. He could smell the elephant herd about half a mile away. He could smell the dust from the plains' animals and—a new smell. What could that be?

He stood very still. There was something on the ground that moved. It was a long long thing and it seemed to move in ripples. Then it curled and uncurled like a long thin trunk.

M'Toto wanted very much to smell it closer but it did not look—friendly. In fact it ran out a long split

tongue and waved it at him. He turned his head to one side as he watched it coil and uncoil, and then the head puffed up and the tongue ran in and out faster and faster. M'Toto sat down and blew some dust at this funny creature.

M'Toto heard his mother calling and for once he answered her immediately. He was sure she could explain this strange trunk that moved by itself and puffed up and stuck a funny-looking tongue in and out.

The Queen followed closely by Aunt Karia crashed through the last of the tall bamboo and thundered down upon the little elephant just as he reached out to touch the stranger. She grabbed him and flung him behind her. Then she shrieked with pain as her trunk was struck by the long, curved fangs. The Queen and Aunt Karia trumpeted long and loudly and then the Queen stomped upon the snake and flung its dead body into the bamboo.

The Queen leaned heavily against a big tree panting and groaning. Aunt Karia again signaled the herd for help and turned to the puzzled little elephant.

"Oh, M'Toto! Your mother has been bitten by a puff adder, a *very* poisonous snake. An elephant's trunk is full of nerves for smelling and feeling and they all go directly to the brain! You—you naughty baby—you could have been KILLED by that snake!"

"Will she—will she—get well?" M'Toto whimpered.

"We will work fast, your mother is strong and healthy." Aunt Karia sighed as she repeated, "We—will work *very* fast!"

The Queen sank down on her knees, her head wavering for a few moments, and then fell heavily to the ground. M'Toto was so very afraid. He crept up against her and nuzzled her with his little head.

Many more aunties rushed to the Queen's side; they touched her gently and grunted in a friendly, reassuring fashion to let her know they were there to help.

"Quickly! Bring me some fresh mud—*hurry!*" Aunt Karia ordered.

One big elephant lashed out with her trunk and spanked M'Toto as he knelt close to his mother's head. "You are a very naughty elephant! Look what pain you have caused your mother. What if she dies? *I* don't want you! Even if you *are* the son of the King!"

Aunt Karia struck the other female. "He is just a baby! He *is* the son of the King! Therefore he must learn many things and most of them he must learn the *hard* way!"

The other elephant dropped her head and stood back as Aunt Karia continued. "Now go with the others, we must work very fast."

The elephants raced to a nearby water hole and worked up mud into large balls and hurried back to the unconscious Queen. Aunt Karia, with her trunk and foot, showed them how to roll the mud into thin pancakes and wrap them around the swollen painful trunk of the Queen.

"This mud will help draw the poison out; we must change it often," she explained.

22

M'Toto again crept close to his mother's head and whispered, "I *am* a naughty elephant—but I love you, Mama! *Please* get well!"

The Queen could not answer. She lay quiet, breathing heavily, her eyes closed. The auntie elephants changed the mud packs every few minutes and M'Toto huddled closer and closer against his sick mother.

The King elephant walked up quietly and M'Toto cowered under his mother's big ear trying to hide. But his father touched him softly on his back and then felt carefully over the head and down the side of the Queen.

"She seems to be breathing easier; keep up the good work. You are all good nurses. We will remain in the bamboo grove tonight; there is plenty of food here for the herd. Tomorrow she will be well enough to travel with us." The King spoke calmly.

Then he turned to Aunt Karia, "Find a nurse for the little one—he will have to be fed also. Tell her the King has ordered it."

So Aunt Karia went through the herd. She found a mother elephant with a baby only a few weeks older than M'Toto and asked her to feed the son of the King until his mother had recovered.

Aunt Hovu and her little female elephant Tana hurried back to the grove with Aunt Karia. Aunt Hovu petted little M'Toto and tried to move him.

But M'Toto would not leave his mother. He whimpered and cried and laid his wet cheek against her hot head. He did not want to eat or even stand up.

Aunt Karia petted him and gently lifted him up and stood him next to Tana. Tana seemed to understand and though she was smaller than M'Toto she put her forehead against his side and pushed and pushed. The mother and auntie elephants stood quietly and watched.

Finally Tana pushed M'Toto under her own mother

and made him drink some milk. It tasted just as good as his own mother's and suddenly he was very hungry—he drank and drank. Then he lay back down by his own mother who seemed to be asleep and nuzzled up under her big ear and sighed.

When M'Toto awakened the following morning his mother was standing. Her trunk hung down to the ground and it was *much* too big. But she *was* standing up, though she moved her great head from side to side as though it pained her very much.

M'Toto hurried to her and pressed his head against her front knee. "Mama?" he whispered. "I'm sorry I slipped away again. I didn't want to *hurt* you." He gently touched her swollen trunk and then buried his head against her knee again.

Aunt Hovu carefully moved him over to her and looked into the Queen's tired eyes.

"I just wonder what he'll think of next!" Aunt Hovu shook her head as M'Toto started to nurse.

"You can be sure it won't be long before he ventures into something else." The Queen spoke with a faint shake of her head.

CHAPTER THREE

M'*Toto and the Big Black Bog*

The herd moved a few miles each day, clearing the forest of the juicy leaves, twigs, and bamboo shoots. Sometimes they had to cross the plains to reach another forest since eighty elephants eat a tremendous amount.

M'Toto and the smallest elephants were herded into the middle of the group as they started their long walk from one forest to another. When the King and his two brothers were satisfied that all were ready they led the way at a brisk pace. At times the weight of the King's nine-foot tusks became too great and tired him. Then his two brothers would walk on either side of him carrying the weight of his tusks on their own trunks to rest the King's neck.

There was no slowing down for the weaker elephants. When M'Toto got tired, which was often, Aunt Karia or his mother would carry him for a way with her trunk. When he was back on his feet again he could not just *walk,* he had to run and tease and pull tails and generally make a big nuisance of himself. He did not like the long walks! No one wanted to stop and play with him.

One day they passed a big, black, muddy water hole with tall reeds growing around it. M'Toto squealed with delight and whirled on his thick little legs and bolted toward the fascinating water. He had now learned to enjoy playing in the pools even though he did not drink water.

His mother grabbed him by an ear and spanked him back in front of her. M'Toto was very puzzled. "Why can't we stop and play in the mud? Why don't you want to take your bath?" he asked his mother.

"Because that is a *bad* pool, M'Toto, we never go near *that* water!" His mother explained.

Other young elephants were being turned back from the tantalizing mud hole by their mothers and aunts and there was a loud uproar all through the herd. But soon all the youngsters were forced back in line and they hurried along. The large elephants passed the water hole without looking back.

M'Toto's lower lip hung down as he pouted. "Why should elephants, the greatest of animals, be afraid of a little old pool of water?"

He lagged behind his mother, frowning and dragging on her tail. He was hot and fretful and as he thought about the cool water a mischievious glint came into his eyes. "I'll fool *them!*" He whispered as he darted under his mother's tall legs and around in front of her.

"Mama? I want to go over and play with Aunt Karia!"

His mother patted him and said, "Don't play too hard; we have a long long walk today!"

28

So M'Toto scampered over to Aunt Karia and pulled her tail. She petted him and asked, "Does your mother know where you are, M'Toto?"

"Oh yes," he said slyly. "I'm going to play with Tana over there!"

Aunt Karia gave him a little slap and said, "Don't play too hard. We have a long walk today."

M'Toto hurried up to Tana and clasped her trunk and they played tug-of-war for a few moments. Then she dropped his trunk and said, "We mustn't play too hard, we have a long walk today."

"Come chase me!" M'Toto called to the other small elephants and darted to the outside of the moving herd.

"We don't want to play. We have a long long walk today!" they called back.

Little M'Toto's lower lip hung farther and farther down as he started to pout again. A big elephant came up and pushed him back into the herd. But as soon as the big one looked away M'Toto stepped quickly into some low bushes and squatted down almost flat. He laid his ear on the ground and listened to the soft rhythmic beat of the herd's feet as they passed him by.

The little elephant must have fallen asleep for a while because when he raised his head to see how far ahead of him the herd was—there were no elephants in sight at all! For a moment he lay there in wonder and then slowly got to his stubby feet.

He threw back his fuzzy little head and snickered.

29

"Haha! I fooled them that time! Now I can do just what I want."

He rolled over in the scrubby grass, pulled up some small flowers and smelled them, then tossed them away. Then he picked some leaves from a low bush and tasted them, but he hurriedly plucked them out of his mouth and

screwed up his face. He wiped his mouth but could not get the bitter taste out of it.

"I'll go back to the water hole and sip some water. I'll have a swim, too! I didn't see anything *bad* about that nice mud hole!" He set off happily, following the trail the elephant herd had left in its wake.

He had almost reached the pool when he heard the cawing of the pesky white egret that always followed the herd. He did not like Zetta! Zetta always screamed at him and had even pecked him once when he had tried to run away.

The bird flew down to him chattering and scolding. M'Toto raised his trunk and blew dust at the egret and shouted teasingly, "You can't carry me, you silly bird! You're too little! Go away!"

The white bird swooped down and again pecked at M'Toto but he only blew more dust into the air. The bird rose high into the air and flew swiftly away in the direction the herd had taken.

M'Toto soon found some "nugu" or monkeys playing under a tree. They leaped around him and onto his back. He was very happy and tried to dance with them and blew more dust high into the air. Suddenly the monkeys stopped playing. They raised their little heads, chattered quickly among themselves and streaked for some big trees near the pool and disappeared into the leaves.

"What did I do? Now I am alone again. Why did they run away from me?" M'Toto wondered aloud.

As M'Toto brooded about the quiet his instinct told him something was wrong. It was so *very* quiet! He lifted his little trunk like a banner but he had filled it so full of dust, blowing it at the bird and monkeys, that he could not smell anything.

He swayed uneasily from side to side. Then he flipped out his hind legs and again started for the pool.

Just then Zetta returned and swooped down to peck him on the head, then the egret let out a loud screech and circled a big thorn tree. M'Toto sat down and rocked merrily back and forth. Zetta screamed louder than ever; she darted at something in the tree and again flew down to the little elephant.

"What does that noisy bird want?" M'Toto wondered.

Then M'Toto noticed something hanging down from the branches of the tree. It looked like a long, round snake but it had big black and orange spots on it. M'Toto got up and walked nearer the tree since his eyes were not very sharp. "That looks like something to play with!"

The strange snaky thing swung back and forth a little faster and Zetta screamed and darted to and fro in great fright. M'Toto looked a little higher into the tree and froze—dead still!

The tail belonged to a *huge* cat! It was all covered with bright orange and black spots. The animal snarled and pulled back its lips and its tail lashed faster and faster.

M'Toto was now very frightened. "It must be a

leopard or a cheetah—I have been warned about them. They eat baby elephants—Aunt Karia told me so!" M'Toto whimpered as the great long fangs of the hungry leopard gleamed in the late afternoon sun.

M'Toto started backing up slowly, slowly, toward the water hole. The bird flew at the leopard and shrieked at the top of her voice. The little elephant trembled with terror. He now knew the bird was trying to protect him. But how could a bird fight a big cat like that?

M'Toto took another step backward and felt the soft mud around his ankle, another step back and the mud was up over both ankles. But something was WRONG with *this* mud! There didn't seem to be any bottom to it. His round baby elephant feet were sinking slowly down— down—*down* into the soft sucking smoothness.

He tried to pull one foot out but it would not move. His front feet were still on dry earth and he leaned forward with all of his strength. But his hind legs refused to move. The black ooze sucked, gurgled, and murmured as he strained to keep his front legs on the dry land.

Panting, he lay down as far as he could on the dry bank and raised his little trunk and shrieked and trumpeted and screamed and cried.

The cat lashed his tail in fury. The egret kept darting at him in swift dives, screaming and calling.

While M'Toto lay panting and crying, his hind legs were sinking deeper and deeper. Now the mud was well over his hips. He trumpeted again and then wound his trunk around a small bush and held on for dear life.

34

With his head pressed against the ground he heard a rumble. He pressed his ear harder against the bank. *Yes!* It was the pounding feet of elephants on the run. Then he heard a trumpet call and then another. He let go of the little bush and bellowed with all his might. He found himself slipping deeper into the mud. This time his trunk would no longer reach the little bush and he grasped for weeds and sticks—*anything* to hold on to.

Zetta was flying in faster circles and calling the elephants to hurry, darting at the angry leopard, and then screeching and darting again.

The leopard lashed his tail and growled, then his tail stiffened out behind him as he sprang down from the tree and with a rush started for M'Toto.

Moving with surprising speed, a great grey form shot into the clearing under the tree. As the leopard sprang for the little elephant the big beast grabbed the huge cat in midair and hurled the thrashing animal into the middle of the great black bog. The leopard screeched and snarled and sank from sight in the thick slimy ooze.

Now the big elephants stormed in from every direction and stopped short swinging their trunks and fanning their great ears as they looked at little M'Toto with just his elbows on the dry bank and the mud almost up to his lower lip.

The elephants seemed to confer with one another for a moment as their trunks touched and their foreheads wrinkled in thought.

The Queen and Aunt Karia moved forward very

slowly. Testing the earth with their great flat feet at every step they found it quivered under their ponderous bodies but did not give way.

M'Toto lifted his little trunk feebly and pleaded with tears in his eyes. "Help me, Mama! Help me, Aunt Karia!"

The Queen reached forward as far as she could and patted him gently on the head. She slowly lowered herself down on her knees and edged forward until she could work her trunk down through the black mud under his forelegs.

Aunt Karia remained standing and stretched out her trunk until she could reach his, then she wrapped her own around his small one and started to pull slowly but steadily. The Queen worked her trunk farther down under his stomach, lifting all the time as she worked.

It seemed to M'Toto that his trunk was going to be pulled right off of his head. The tears ran down his cheeks but he did not make a sound except a gasp through his open mouth.

Now his hips were free of the sloppy mud and slowly, oh so slowly out came one small leg and then another.

Still on her knees the Queen carefully edged back from the quaking bog, lifting her little son as Aunt Karia steadily pulled on his trunk.

With a gurgling-sucking sigh his mud-caked legs came free! The auntie quickly flung him on to safe ground.

Together the four-ton females moved slowly and carefully backward, the queen on her knees while Aunt Karia

placed each foot with great care upon the quivering earth. As soon as the auntie felt the solid earth under her feet she slipped her strong trunk under the head of the Queen and helped her to her feet.

The great bog, with its bottomless depth, had been defeated this time after centuries of swallowing all great and small animals that had unwarily stepped upon its tempting bank.

All the elephants withdrew to safer ground. The King found a small spring and drawing up the water into his trunk sprayed the little elephant while the Queen and the auntie rubbed him clean. All the time they worked they grunted soothingly to the trembling youngster.

M'Toto kept his head down. He swayed with fatigue and fright and was so *very* ashamed of what he had done. He knew that both his mother and auntie had risked their lives for him. He had felt the earth tremble and sway when they were pulling him out.

And any one of the elephants could have been terribly clawed by that hungry leopard.

"We will rest here tonight; there is enough food for us and we will join the others at daybreak," the King ordered.

M'Toto rolled his head a little to one side and peered shyly up at the King of the elephants. The King looked at the little elephant for a long time and then raised his trunk. M'Toto dropped his head quickly. He knew he deserved a good thrashing and braced himself to receive

38

it. But the wise, gentle King touched M'Toto lightly and tweaked his ear.

"How—did you know?" M'Toto asked his father in a small voice.

"Zetta, our lookout, brought word to us that you were in trouble. *I*—would not have come back for *one* very naughty little elephant. The WHOLE herd is my responsibility! But, your mother and aunties and Zetta— whom you dislike—insisted on trying to save you. I sent the rest of the herd along with my brothers. But *next* time, my son——!" The King's voice stopped and he stared hard at the baby elephant.

M'Toto shivered and crept under his mother and peeked out between her front legs at the King.

The King pulled the corners of his mouth down and tried very hard to scowl at the baby elephant, but he could not help touching the little one again lightly as he said, "Now—will you follow your leader?"

"Oh *yes*, good King! Oh *yes*, Father! I'll always follow YOU!" And he meant it sincerely—at that moment.

CHAPTER FOUR

M'*Toto Meets the Ants*

The heavy spring rains of former years had been much lighter this year and the summer showers had held little moisture for the parched earth. And now that fall was here the sun still glared down upon the brown landscape.

For many weeks the herd had traveled from one forest to another. The long drought and careless feeding habits of elephants had destroyed much of the forests. Their huge bodies each demanded a half a ton of food a day. M'Toto and the other young elephants did not worry since they still nursed, but their mothers worried! And the King was greatly troubled about his herd. The big elephants were hungry!

M'Toto felt the tension in the air and watched and listened as the King and his brothers conferred. They studied the great trees that were heavy with leaves at the top. But no branches had grown back on the lower trunks of the trees and the elephants could not reach the food they needed so badly.

"We must push over a big tree so the herd can eat!" the King declared.

"We will help, Brother. But they must be made to

eat *every* leaf and twig! It seems we are fast running out of forests!" his brothers replied.

The three great elephants selected the tree and put their foreheads against the rough bark and pushed and pushed. The tree that had stood for a hundred years leaned farther and farther and finally fell with a great crash.

The huge roots of the tree towered thirty feet in the air, dwarfing the huge animals. Many insects had been hidden beneath it; now they ran out in every direction. The elephants were delighted and caught and ate the insects with relish.

M'Toto had watched with excitement as the King and his brothers pushed over the great tree and was now frisking about behind them. Suddenly Busia, the younger of the King's brothers, let out a scream, then a mighty trumpet call and started running around and around. He ran in figure eights, beating his trunk against the ground, snorting, blowing, running, and crying.

M'Toto rolled on the ground and laughed and laughed. He kicked his round feet in the air and beat his little trunk on the ground and choked on his laughter. It was a very funny sight. *Very* funny!

After his frantic running and trumpeting and thrashing his trunk around, Busia stampeded across the veldt at an astounding speed toward a water hole.

M'Toto rocked and laughed and rocked and laughed.

It was such a funny thing for a dignified elephant to do—suddenly to start acting so oddly. M'Toto laughed until the tears ran down his cheeks.

Aunt Karia poked him with her trunk. "Do not laugh so much! It is *not* funny! 'Safari' or 'Driver' ants can crawl up inside an elephant's trunk and drive him frantic!"

"I thought it was *very* funny! He was having such a good time!" M'Toto chuckled, as usual not listening to his aunt.

"He was not having a *good* time! And you stay away from those tree roots!" His auntie ordered.

As Aunt Karia moved off to the head of the fallen tree to get her share of the food, little M'Toto sat chuckling to himself. "Tree roots? So that's what made him so funny. I will have to find out why."

The elephants were all so busy filling their long-empty stomachs that no one paid any attention to the baby elephant. He passed under the great beasts, between their legs and sauntered back to have a look at the tree roots. He had not yet learned his lesson to *listen* to the elders' advice.

Like any other elephant, M'Toto's eyesight was not very good, so he used his trunk to tell him about all the things in front of him. M'Toto could see the big roots ten times taller than he was, but he could not see anything that would interest an *elephant!*

So he sniffed here and he sniffed there. He touched and smelled and felt and snuffed. All at once he felt a sting up in his trunk. Then another—and *another*—and ANOTHER! He blew through his trunk with all his might but the stinging grew worse and *worse* and WORSE!

He screamed in panic and started to run in circles and beat his little trunk on the ground. Tears ran out of his eyes so thickly he could not see where he was going.

He ran into bushes and into tree trunks. He ran into elephant legs and into shrubs and brambles. He screamed and trumpeted again and again. Suddenly he was lifted off of the ground and elephant feet thundered out across the veldt with him struggling and crying in the grasp of a big trunk. The stinging was way up inside his trunk, almost to his eyes. He cried and squealed but his cries grew weaker and fainter.

All at once he was plopped down in a water hole. "Suck up the water and mud and blow it out—*quickly!*" His mother ordered.

He felt very weak but tried to do as his mother told him. The water hurt! The mud hurt! He blew it all out.

"Again! Do it again, M'Toto!"

This time it did not hurt quite so badly. "Draw it up farther into your trunk!" His mother shook him to make him obey.

Again and again M'Toto drew the water and mud

into his trunk and blew it out. He could not see the little
ants that tumbled out of his trunk in the stream of muddy
water. He only knew that the stinging—that awful pain—
was slowly going away.

He was *so* tired. He leaned against his mother's big
legs and the tears ran down his cheeks. She rubbed him
and held him closely.

"Feeling better, little son?" she asked gently.

He rubbed his furry, stubborn little head against her
leg and whimpered.

"All right, take hold of my tail and we will go back
to the herd. I must eat my dinner!" the Queen said.

"Can't you carry me?" M'Toto asked, still leaning
heavily against her front leg.

"I can*not* carry you! You are much too heavy!"

"But you carried me down here, didn't you?" M'Toto
begged.

"I did indeed! But only because you were in so much
pain. You can walk back to the forest all right."

"But—you *did*—carry me!" whined M'Toto, nuzzling
up to his mother.

The Queen grew impatient with her naughty little son
and she was also very hungry. She spanked him with her
trunk on his little rump. "Take hold of my tail! We are
going back to the herd!"

"It hurts, Mama, it hurts!"

"Of course it hurts! You thought it very funny when

Busia got ants up his trunk. Now you whimper and cry. I'm ashamed of you—the son of the *King!*"

The Queen walked back to the forest very slowly. She ate everything she could find along the way, pushing M'Toto in front of her since she realized it did hurt him to use his trunk.

M'Toto did not look up, he kept his head down and his swollen trunk dragged in the sand. When they reached the herd he felt a soft touch on his head and then another and another. Every elephant that they passed touched him gently in sympathy.

When they had cleaned every leaf, twig and tender bark from the great tree the King ordered the elephants back to the water hole. "Now you must eat all of the reeds and water hyacinths you can hold. We must travel tonight toward the bamboo groves. There is no water until we reach the mountains and it will take us all night and all day to get there. So fill your stomachs as full of food and water as you can."

"The King is very worried, isn't he?" Aunt Karia asked the Queen.

"*Very* worried! The forests are so dry and barren because of the lack of rainfall. He fears we may starve before the fall rains begin," the Queen answered.

"And there is no sign of their beginning!" Aunt Karia shook her massive head. "May I take care of M'Toto for a while? I know you are tired and hungry."

"You may indeed! He has been a very naughty little elephant—again!" answered the Queen gratefully.

Aunt Karia tilted M'Toto's head up and looked into his swollen eyes. She took his trunk carefully in hers and examined it closely.

"I will carry you for a little way, M'Toto. You are too heavy to carry very far, but I know you do not feel very well." She lifted him up around his fat little middle and he promptly went to sleep, his sore trunk dangling limply.

As the dusk settled over the African veldt the King rounded up his herd and started them on their long hard walk through the dark night.

CHAPTER FIVE

M'*Toto Meets the Dik Dik*

The new day found the herd many miles from their own forest. The brush was dry and crackled as they swiftly pushed their way along. As the heat became more intense they were forced to seek relief. On this route the few pools, where they had formerly bathed, were mere mud holes but the great beasts found enough moisture by digging deep with their powerful trunks to slake their thirst and spray their hot bodies.

M'Toto and the other babies were well smeared with cool mud to keep them from sunstroke as they continued their hurried trip across the wide plains which led to the mountains where the bamboo grew.

When they reached the foothills the trail looked steep and dangerous but the elephant path had been used for thousands of years and was worn smooth.

Here the roaring rivers were now only murmuring streams but the water was fresh and each elephant stopped in the narrow mountain path to drink deeply and spray his body again and again. The little ones protested the cold showers with a clamor of trumpet shrieks and whimpering cries. But their need for the moisture was even greater than the big elephants'.

The soft pads of the little ones were blistered and swollen from the long hot journey. M'Toto whined and begged to be carried, but the uphill trail was slow enough for the weakest ones to follow so the Queen and the aunties refused to carry the little elephant. Holding onto the tail of his mother or an auntie M'Toto grumbled at every steep step.

He slipped from the path to hide behind a large tree trunk to take a nap, but his mother felt him let go of her tail and called back to Aunt Karia who followed right behind her. Aunt Karia spotted his baggy little bottom under the branches and slapped him back onto the path.

"M'Toto, you stay in line or you're really going to be spanked!" his auntie scolded him.

"But I am so *tired!*" M'Toto cried.

"We are *all* tired! We will rest when we reach the bamboos."

"I don't want any bamboo! I want to rest *now!*" M'Toto argued.

"Do you want to be left in this great dry forest by yourself?" Aunt Karia asked.

M'Toto thought about the day he had run away and was nearly attacked by the leopard.

"No-o-o-o. But—I'm TIRED!" he said fretfully.

"We are nearly there, M'Toto. We will be able to eat and rest in a little while. The trail is too steep to carry you. Be a good little elephant. Make the King proud that you are his son," the auntie pleaded.

"Make the King proud! Make the King proud! *Make the King proud!*" M'Toto said the words over and over to himself as he lifted each tired little foot and put it in front of the other. "I'll make them *all* proud of me! But—I am *so* tired!"

M'Toto heard strange noises from way up ahead. A snapping and crackling and smashing. He shook his heavy little head and raised his ears and trunk. What was that noise? "Aunt Karia?" He jerked her tail.

"Yes, M'Toto, we have almost reached the bamboo. The first elephants in the line are eating already. That is what you hear. We eat the tender tips that grow way up high and then tear up the roots and eat them too. They are very good!"

"Can I eat some?" M'Toto puffed.

"No, not for quite a while yet. Maybe in a year or two you will be able to eat it."

"Why?" Like all young things M'Toto was full of "whys."

"You do not have teeth with which to chew the bamboo," his mother answered. Turning part way around in the steep trail she lifted M'Toto and swung him up and around in front of her. She tapped the auntie in front of her. Aunt Koma turned and grasped him with her trunk and swung him up ahead of her. Then, one after the other, the elephants reached behind and swung M'Toto up and up and up the trail until he felt as if he were in a swift river current.

He was finally placed on his feet right behind the King and his brothers who were already in the tall bamboo eating. The King turned around and looked at him sternly and fanned his great ears. "What are *you* doing up here, M'Toto?"

"I—I don't know, Sir. I was swung up here by many elephant trunks," M'Toto answered, his head down for fear he had done something to anger the King.

"Were you bothering the other elephants?" The King frowned.

"Y-e-s-s Sir, I guess I was. I didn't mean to, I was just so very tired."

"We are all tired, my son. We must be patient with one another. Stand over there by that stream until your Mother arrives," ordered the King. "You can rest safely there."

The big elephants moved away and slowly ate their way through the dense bamboo forest, clearing all before them.

M'Toto moved over to the small stream as he had been ordered and drowsily watched it as it ran in gurgles and gobbles and giggles, over small stones and through moss, under branches and around rocks. A small fish darted out from under a stone, grabbed a morsel of food and darted back.

M'Toto sat down by the stream and trailed his small trunk in the cool water. He grabbed at the little fish with the fingers of his trunk but he was still too young to use them well. Finally he laid his tired heavy head against a big boulder so he could watch the fish with more comfort and the brook rippled and twinkled and sparkled and seemed to sing a lullaby. M'Toto closed his eyes and fell asleep.

"H-e-l-l-O. Who are you?" The voice was young and very soft.

M'Toto opened his sleepy eyes. Two big brown eyes with two long tan ears were peering closely at him.

M'Toto yawned and tried to raise his tired head from the boulder.

The little creature darted into a bush, then carefully step by step came out again.

"Who—are—you?" This time the question was only in a whisper.

M'Toto sighed. "I am M'Toto, son of the King elephant and—I am *very* tired!" Then mimicking the speech of the tiny antelope he said. "Who—are—you?"

"I am Mydac! The son of the dik diks!"

M'Toto's trunk trailed back into the water and an impish gleam came into his eyes as he sucked up some water and mischievously sprayed it on the small creature.

In a flash he was alone again.

"Mydac! Mydac? Come back. I'm sorry, I didn't mean to frighten you!" M'Toto pushed himself up to a sitting position and curled his trunk under his chin and then into his mouth and sucked on it a few moments.

There was a rustle of leaves and two big eyes looked

out from under a small bush. "You—blew—*water*—on me!" The little dik dik stated with great indignation.

"I'm sorry! Please come out and talk to me!" M'Toto was wide awake now and very curious.

As the dik dik stepped slowly from the cover of the bushes, M'Toto said, "My, but you are tiny! Were you just born?" M'Toto turned his head to one side studying the little antelope that stood only twelve inches high at the shoulder. Mydac's large brown eyes and long ears made him look like a jackrabbit.

"Goodness *no!* I'm a whole YEAR old! I'm full grown!"

"You mean you won't be any bigger—ever?" M'Toto was astonished by these strange facts.

"Of course not! We don't want to be! We live in the desert and hide under the thorn bushes. We can run like the dust devils!" The dik dik pranced on his hind legs and turned around and around. "I don't weigh as much as that long long nose of yours!"

"Why should you be so proud of that?" M'Toto asked, thinking how much finer it was to be a big elephant.

"Because I can run and leap five times my height, I can turn and spin on a pebble. And I can hide under a small pile of grass!" Mydac leaped into the air, sprang across the stream, darted under a bush, and then leaped back in front of the little elephant.

"Isn't all that very tiring?" M'Toto was still weary from the long long walk and all that racing and jumping just made him want to go back to sleep.

"But how do you escape *your* enemies?" Mydac asked bewildered.

"Enemies? I didn't know I had any! Oh, except— the lions, the leopard and the snake." M'Toto leaned back against the boulder to think this over.

"Lion? Leopard? Snake? Haven't you ever met the crocodile? The cheetah? Or—the rhino yet?"

"No, I don't think so, should I?" M'Toto asked innocently.

"Should you? I should hope not! You haven't got the sense yet to get out of the way of a worm!" Mydac shook his small head and his topknot waved.

"Worm? Like this one?" M'Toto gently picked up an earthworm from the bank of the stream and turned it around to his eyes and then held it out to the dik dik.

"Disgusting! What if that was a baby adder? He could bite you!" Mydac said, mincing out of reach.

"But," M'Toto carefully laid the worm back on the

bank where he had found him. "That *isn't* an adder. I *have* met one of them!" And he nodded his head knowingly.

"What do you call that long nose that moves around by itself?" Mydac's curiosity was overcoming his nervousness.

"Haven't you ever seen elephants before?" M'Toto turned his trunk around to his eye, studying it as though he had never noticed it before.

"Not closely. I come from far away, clear out in the desert! But I have seen the big ones moving through the bush and under the trees in the forest. I just never *met* one before.

M'Toto finished his inspection of his own trunk and then proudly stated. "This is my TRUNK! It can do just about anything. When I get stronger I could pick you up and throw you clear over this mountain!"

"Why would you want to do that?" Mydac began edging away again.

"Because you woke me up! Besides, it just might be fun!" M'Toto boasted.

"You have a hole in the end of that—that *trunk?* Mydac was inspecting the strange snout with interest.

"Of course! I can breathe through it and suck up water. I can call through it like a trumpet! See?" M'Toto blew a squeaky little trumpet call through it. "I'll bet you can't do anything like *that!*"

A great commotion was heard in the bamboo behind

them. Aunt Karia, the Queen, and several other aunties thundered over to the baby elephant. In a flash the little antelope had jumped the stream and disappeared.

"What's wrong, M'Toto? Why did you call for help?" The Queen asked him worriedly.

"Nothing is wrong, Mama. I was just showing off my trunk to my new little friend, Mydac the dik dik!"

"There's no one here, M'Toto. You must have been dreaming. Besides,dik diks only live in the desert."

"He *was* here! Right here! You scared him away!"

The big elephants swung their trunks over the ground and bushes. "Yes, he was here!" The Queen said to the aunties. "I wonder why he is so far from his home?"

"Mydac! Mydac! Please come and meet my mama and aunties. They won't hurt you. Please come out and meet them!" M'Toto called.

A small bush rustled across the stream, then a tiny head appeared under a branch. The head lowered and two little horns stood out between Mydac's big ears as though he were going to charge the massive elephants.

"Good day to you, little dik dik. What are you doing so far away from the desert?" The Queen spoke softly to the tiny animal.

"Haven't you heard of the great fire?" Mydac's voice quivered from his anxiety.

"Fire?" whispered the female elephants, looking at each other in an anxious manner.

"Is *fire* bad?" M'Toto asked bewildered.

60

"Haven't you seen the animals that are hurrying over this mountain?" Mydac asked.

"I'm afraid we haven't noticed, we have been hungry for a long while and eighty elephants crashing around in bamboo makes it hard to hear other noises," the Queen replied.

"Perhaps they are using the game trails that are a little farther on," said Aunt Karia.

"Let's go tell my father, the King! He will want to know if something *bad* is near!" M'Toto scrambled awkwardly to his stumpy legs. "Follow me, Mydac. I'll take you to the King."

CHAPTER SIX

The Forest Fire

The little elephant hurried through the large herd that was noisily feeding on the bamboo. The tiny dik dik followed him in leaps and bounds. M'Toto felt very important and was eager to give his father the news and to introduce his new friend, Mydac.

But when M'Toto and the tiny dik dik reached him, the King was busily stuffing bamboo into his mouth and did not hear—or care to listen—to the chatter of the baby elephant. M'Toto called again and again and finally tapped his foot sharply and impatiently upon the big elephant's sensitive toenails. Mydac peeked out timidly from under M'Toto's body.

The King, annoyed, looked down. He stopped eating and turned his great head sideways so his big ear dropped nearer his son. "What is it, M'Toto? Why did you step on my toenails? That is a very rude thing to do!"

"I'm sorry, Father, but you must listen. We have been told by Mydac, the dik dik, that there is a great *fire* coming up the mountain. Isn't that right, Mydac?" M'Toto peered under his stomach at the tiny animal crouched there.

"Fire? Isn't that just the smoke from the autumn grass fires that we have been smelling?" The King lowered his head farther and stared at the little antelope.

"No, Your Honor. Many of the deer, buffalo, gazelles, and other prairie dwellers have already crossed over this mountain to the plains on the other side. Even the lions and hyenas have hurried through, not stopping to eat. *We* are all afraid, shouldn't you be?"

"Let me talk with my brothers, we did not know it was so serious," the King answered.

"But it *must* rain! The fall rains are weeks past due and the clouds are heavy with moisture!" exclaimed one brother.

"And if it does not rain?" The King hesitated for a moment. "We are on a crest of a mountain, if the fire should come up both sides— we would not have a chance."

"What do *you* suggest? You are our leader," his other brother asked him.

"We will watch closely. I think we had better remain here for as long as we can. If the rains come we are saved. If they don't come we will have to bolt through the burning forest. Then only the fastest elephants—will live."

Even as the elephants heard the news of the great fire and planned what they would do the bamboo seemed to come alive with other fleeing animals. The antelope and gazelles sailed by apparently without touching the earth, their high jumps and leaps carrying them swiftly out of sight, only their white tails visible as they waved a warning of trouble behind.

A large group of giraffe seldom seen in the steep mountain areas clumped past in their rocking-horse gait.

Their long necks thrust high above the bamboo and their large dark eyes stared in fright.

A pair of cheetahs streaked past and even the cape buffalo thundered by in a massed herd, their black nostrils distended and eyes glassy with fear.

The King elephant and his brothers kept the herd tightly together. There was much uneasiness among them but they continued to eat and drink and obey their leader. They had been hungry a long time and would soon need all of their strength. The small stream was clear and clean and though not large enough for the elephants to lie down in they could drink all they needed and spray the water over their bodies again and again.

From under the safety of the big Queen's stomach, M'Toto and Mydac watched as a small herd of black rhino came over the crest of the mountain. Snorting and pawing they stopped and faced the elephants and lowered their heads as if for battle. They did not like the elephants and the elephants did not like the black rhino. But only the rhino would be foolish enough to stop for battle in this dangerous area.

The great animals faced each other squarely. The King and his brothers stood close together. Their big bodies swung loosely as they shifted their weight from leg to leg. Their trunks were held stiffly in front of them, then curled under their lips and then out again. The great ears fanned forward and held tense and then folded flat against their heads as though they were about to charge.

The rhino also shifted their dangerous bulk from leg to leg. The long horns on their noses pointed directly at the King elephant and their mean little eyes flickered and grew redder as their anger increased.

Finally the King spoke. "Pass over the mountains, brothers of the forest. But I feel it is to your death!"

"*Our* death?" Snorted the leader of the rhinos. "The fire is *behind* us! But it is climbing fast! Do you think you and your herd can blow it out with your puny trunks?"

The King and his brothers put their trunks into the air like periscopes. "It is indeed close but a storm is also very close. The fires have encircled this mountain by now. There *is* no escape without the rain—except to dash

through the flames to the burned-out areas. We will remain here."

The rhinos snorted in contempt and trotted off in a compact group down the other side of the mountain.

M'Toto felt his tiny friend trembling at his side. "If only I could see over this bamboo, I might be able to find a way out. You elephants have a fine sense of smell but we dik diks can see for miles!" Mydac whispered.

"Maybe I can lift you up!" M'Toto darted out from under his mother and tried to raise the little antelope over his head but his trunk was still too weak.

The King frowned down at M'Toto. "What are you trying to do with your little friend? You'll hurt him! Put him down!"

"But he can see so *very* far and we can't! If he could see over this bamboo maybe he could find a way out!" M'Toto argued, carefully placing Mydac back on solid ground.

The great elephant stared silently at the baby elephant and the tiny dik dik. He moved his big body slowly from side to side and thought deeply.

"You may be right, son. If the dik dik could see over this bamboo perhaps he *could* help us find a way to safety."

The dik dik crept back under M'Toto and peered out with wide frightened eyes at the great beast that was standing so quietly by them.

"Would you help us, Mydac?" the King asked, as he softly touched the timid little animal. "I can easily lift

you high over the bamboo. I will be very careful, I promise you."

"Please, Mydac!" M'Toto begged, touching his little friend. "Please do what my father asks. He will not hurt you!"

With quivering legs the dik dik slowly stepped out in front of the big elephant. The King carefully raised him straight over his head until he was far, far from the ground.

M'Toto watched in awe as the little dik dik first shuddered with eyes shut tight, then bravely he raised his little head and strained his eyes in each direction.

"I guess being that small must be pretty nice at that!" said M'Toto, turning to his mother. "I wish I were a dik dik!"

The Queen pushed him back under her with a chuckle. "Now wouldn't I look silly being the mother of a dik dik? You *must* stay under me, M'Toto, so no sparks will fall on you."

"Can you see over the bamboo? Can you see through the smoke, Mydac?" The King asked anxiously.

"Yes! I can occasionally get a clear view." And the little dik dik described what he could see. "There are the red lines of fire creeping up both sides of the mountain. The big trees burst into flame with a savage roar. The steam rises in clouds from the small streams that are boiling. *And*—at the far left—there is a break in the red lines——like a long passage.!"

The King carefully set Mydac back on the ground.

M'Toto rushed to him and held him closely against his
knees for a moment. "What did you see, Mydac? Could
you really see all of that wonderful sight?"

"Yes, little elephant, I saw all of that—and I also saw
a *very* strange thing!"

"What?" The King almost shook the tiny animal in
his anxiety.

"To the left, from the direction the wind is blowing there is a long strip of brown, it is *not* on fire. It is as wide as a river but it is *not* a river. I do not know what it is—but it is *not* on fire!"

"Move into the wind!" The King trumpeted to his herd. He turned to touch the little dik dik. "Thank you, Mydac. And please stay close to M'Toto, we may need your wonderful eyesight again."

The herd moved in orderly fashion into the wind. They still fed hungrily on the bamboo and between mouthfuls their trunks were constantly sampling the air to make sure they were progressing in the right direction. The smoke and ashes grew more intense. There were cries and trumpet shrieks of pain as a burning cinder or branch landed on a broad sensitive back.

The King held his head high into the wind, feeling it with his trunk. "What do you see now, Mydac?" He asked without thinking.

"Elephant feet and bamboo stubble!" M'Toto shouted with laughter. "What do you think a tiny creature *could* see when he doesn't even reach your knees, Father?"

The King poked his laughing son in the ribs. Then he peered under M'Toto at the little dik dik. "Mydac, as a dik dik you pride yourself on your sense of balance, do you not?"

"Of course! We can balance on a rolling rock or a pebble! We are very agile!" the dik dik answered, with a flip of his forelock.

72

Then you will have no difficulty at all riding on my broad head." The King stated.

"On *your—HEAD?* Oh, no! You are much *too* tall! I could never stand that height!" Mydac answered in shocked terror.

"Little dik dik, you have just climbed this mountain by yourself. It is at least *5,000* feet higher than your desert home. I am only eleven feet higher!" the King explained kindly.

The little antelope's eyes were wide with wonder. "*I* climbed 5,000 feet? I can hardly believe it! You are sure that you're just—*eleven* feet tall?"

"I'm sure, Mydac, and I will treat you with great care," the King said as he again lifted the tiny animal, placing him carefully on his broad smooth head. But the dik dik trembled and shook—and *shooook*—and *shooooook!* His legs wilted under him and in complete terror he sank down between the great ears of the elephant.

The King could feel the little antelope trembling so he touched him gently now and then with his trunk. "Mydac, you need not be ashamed of being frightened. You came up the mountain one small dik dik step at a time. Now you have been lifted eleven feet into the air all at *once.* Lie quietly, little friend, until you feel secure again."

CHAPTER SEVEN

The Flooded Canyon

The King elephant and his brothers quickly guided the herd through the bamboo groves, through the smoke and sparks and burning branches, and on toward the left where the little antelope had thought he had seen a break in the great fires.

M'Toto reluctantly stayed under his mother though it was hard walking sideways with his head out from under her so he could keep his eye on Mydac.

"Why doesn't he stand up, Mama? Is he sick?" M'Toto asked anxiously.

"I expect he is a little 'sick,' M'Toto. Don't worry he will do his part when he is needed," the Queen reassured the worried baby elephant.

She clasped M'Toto's trunk in hers to keep him close. The sparks from the forest fire fell faster and faster and she feared his tender young skin would receive a bad burn.

"Can you see everything up there, Mydac?" M'Toto shouted.

"It is difficult, little elephant. The smoke from the fires is very dense and when it clears for a moment the bamboos close over me again. Next time we reach a clear spot, perhaps the King could lift me up a few feet higher." Mydac whistled down to the little elephant.

"I'll be happy to, Mydac," the King interrupted. "I'm glad you are no longer afraid."

"Oh, I wouldn't say *that!*" Mydac smiled down at M'Toto. "But if I cannot save you, then—I cannot save myself."

M'Toto watched a little enviously as Mydac stood up, balancing himself gracefully as the King elephant hurried along coaxing the herd to greater speed.

"Now! Lift me up now, great King!" the dik dik whistled.

The King stopped and lifted Mydac high into the air. Then the King started slowly to raise up on his hind legs but could not get his balance on the uneven ground.

M'Toto hurriedly dropped his mother's trunk and raced out in front of the King. "Balance yourself on my back, Father! I'm not afraid!"

The King smiled proudly to himself as M'Toto backed up to him and stood very still. He placed one great foot lightly on his little son's back and stretched his trunk high into the air to give the dik dik the best view possible.

"We are almost to the break! It starts down hill very suddenly! I do not know what it is, but—it is *not* on fire!" the dik dik whistled.

"It is a canyon—a great gorge! Now I remember! Do we dare take the herd in there?" Busia asked his brother the King. "I was down that great gorge many years ago. It is very steep! I fear some of the old elephants and very young elephants will not be able to make it down!"

"But look behind you!" Brother Gatto said. "The bamboo is now in flames! Though the thunder rolls and the lighting flashes there is still not a drop of rain!"

"You are so right, Gatto. We must fight to survive or stand still and die," said the King.

"Call the strongest of the aunties and some of the young bulls to start the descent, then the mothers, babies, and older elephants. Gatto, you lead! Busia, you follow up the rear with the other young and strong ones to help those that get into trouble!" The King shouted his orders.

Just as the King set Mydac back on the ground a young bull elephant bellowed in frenzy when a burning spark lit on his back. He wheeled around in a circle trumpeting wildly and stampeded past the King. Mydac was knocked through the air and fell heavily on the sharp bamboo stubble.

M'Toto again scrambled out from under his mother and ran to his little friend's side. *"Mydac!* You've been hurt!" M'Toto carefully picked the little dik dik up and carried him back to the protection under his mother.

The King was much too busy to notice what had happened as many of the elephants were panicking.

M'Toto carried the little dik dik, whose legs hung limply. One foot was bleeding badly. The tears ran out of M'Toto's eyes and dripped off his curled trunk, dampening the body of the unconscious little animal.

As M'Toto and his mother reached the brink of the

deep canyon, she tried to make him lay the little dik dik down on the edge. But M'Toto wailed so loudly and rebelled so strongly against making the slide down into the gorge without the dik dik that a very quick conference had to be held among the aunties.

"He saved our lives! We can't just leave him!" Aunt Karia said, shaking her great head.

"But I cannot manage an injured antelope and take care of M'Toto too. *He* could not carry that little creature ten feet in this canyon, then it would surely be trampled." The Queen argued, since she had all she could worry about with her own baby.

M'Toto stubbornly closed his eyes and held on to the limp little body. "If *he* doesn't go—*I* won't go!"

"Give him to me, M'Toto! I will carry him for you. But if his leg is broken he will not survive anyway," Aunt Koma said. She gently loosened M'Toto's hold on the dik dik and gathered him up and slid down the canyon holding Mydac over her head.

The mother elephants and their young as well as their helpers, the aunties, followed the younger and stronger scouts into the narrow pass and slowly, ponderously stepped and slid over and around the huge boulders. Occasionally the baby elephants had to be lifted from rock to rock when it was too dangerous for them or when they were in danger of being trampled.

M'Toto tried very hard to be brave but he was a very frightened baby elephant and he squealed his fright *very* often.

The leaders when faced with a steep incline sat back on their haunches and slid to the bottom of the drop. After ten or twelve had made the slide it was in better condition for the smaller and weaker ones.

The fires were now roaring above them but there was no forest growth in the dry canyon to catch fire, for a while they seemed to be safe.

The wind blew up the gorge in a gale carrying dirt, sand, and ashes. The smoke was so intense at times it was almost impossible to see even a few steps in front as the animals struggled to keep their footing in the steep pass.

M'Toto cried and hung on to first his mother and when she became exhausted he held on to Aunt Karia and then Aunt Koma who was carrying Mydac, the dik dik. The big leaders would slide down a steep place and then stop to help the next ones.

The burning sparks and cinders showered down on them and the elephants screamed in pain and bellowed in rage at the enemy they could not reach.

Suddenly the thunder rolled louder than ever and lightning flashed up and down the canyon. At last the rains came down. Not just rain but torrents of water poured over them, cooling their burning skins.

M'Toto promptly stopped in the narrow path and wanted to cool himself in the rapidly forming pools and streams. His mother quickly grabbed him out of the way of those following and held him closely to her.

The King and the other elephants were now more worried by the rains than they had been by the fires. Hordes of other animals had followed the elephants, from the ill-tempered rhinos to little field mice. These canyons with straight high cliffs on either side had been cut deep into the earth by many other floods for hundreds of years. Was there any way out for them when the flood waters hit?

A frenzied rhino charged by, shoving the Queen into a deep hole and she lost her hold on M'Toto.

M'Toto was now too frightened to cry out. The water washed under his short legs and swung him around against the big legs of Aunt Koma. He grabbed her tail and was swished this way and that. Holding the dik dik over her head she could not grasp the floundering baby elephant.

The bellowing of terrified animals made the canyon ring and echo with cries of fright and pain. They were washed around corners of huge boulders into deep pools so suddenly they just swam furiously in any direction. When one animal would reach a small sandbar, ten others would frantically try to climb upon it, pushing one another off in their panic.

Still, the water rose higher and higher. A black wave struck M'Toto, he lost his grip on his auntie's tail and tumbled end over end like a rubber ball down a waterfall and came bobbing to the top screeching with all his might.

Swimming rapidly the Queen caught up with him and again held him closely to her. But the struggle was tiring

her rapidly and she shoved him onto a big boulder to rest.

Aunt Karia picked him up to guide him for a little way but just then another great wave of muddy water came down the gorge and rolled them both over and over and over.

Aunt Karia's long legs finally found secure ground under the raging water, but M'Toto rolled on and on down the rampaging river around a corner and out of sight.

The Queen, Aunt Karia, and other aunties trumpeted and bellowed and tried to catch up with the baby elephant that bobbed and swirled and ducked from sight in the roiling waters.

As they swam frantically around a bend a young bull trumpeted, "M'Toto is over there on the other side of the canyon! He's caught in some drift wood. It is *very* deep water, can you get him over to this sand bar?"

"I will help!" Aunt Koma called as she laid the injured dik dik on a high point of land and joined the Queen and Aunt Karia.

M'Toto floated and bobbed helplessly in the tangle of drift wood. He sent out one terrified shriek after another. The rough branches scratched and beat about his small body as he tried to clutch them for support. He was tossed up and down against the cliff face as wave after wave swirled around him.

The tide of animals going down the flood waters was growing greater and greater. Lions, giraffe, rhino, and deer of all kinds. Everything living that had escaped the inferno above was now fighting for life in the flooded gorge.

The Queen and her helpers edged their way into the swift stream, dodging the other struggling animals as they tried to make their way to M'Toto.

The King swam in view of the floundering females and at once saw the difficulty. He trumpeted to other big elephants and they closed in. Each caught the tail of another with his trunk and swung himself out into the flood to form a dam. The females could now swim to M'Toto and bring him back safely to the point of land on which the dik dik had been placed.

Other animals in the rushing water crawled up on the great elephants as though they were islands in that raging water. None was pushed away.

The Queen and her helpers reached the tired, half-drowned little elephant and putting their trunks under his front legs they lifted him almost out of the water as they swam back to the sandbar and placed him beside the dik dik.

Mydac lay watching as they put the baby elephant down by him. Then the big females formed a solid circle against this small point of land so other animals could not crowd upon it.

The baby elephant lay shivering, eyes tightly closed. Mydac did not try to stand but pulled his little body over to M'Toto's head and licked his eyebrow.

"Is he hurt badly?" the dik dik asked the Queen.

"I don't think so. He's been very frightened and he

probably swallowed a good deal of that muddy water," she answered.

Again Mydac licked the eyelid of the little elephant.

M'Toto opened his eye and stared at the little antelope. He touched the dik dik with his trunk. "You're Mydac, aren't you?"

"Yes, how are you feeling?"

"I—I'm all right I guess." Then M'Toto remembered how Mydac had been hurt. "What about you? Let me look at your leg!" M'Toto rolled over onto his knees and felt along the injured leg of the dik dik.

The Queen and aunties smiled with relief at M'Toto's sudden recovery when he had something besides himself to worry about.

The King moved over to the huddle and looked at the two young ones so interested in one another. Mydac glanced up in time to see a faint smile on the great elephant's face.

"Oh, Your Honor! Some antelope spoke to me while I waited here. This is the mouth of a small ravine that leads up to the grassland. They said we could climb it when the rain stops."

"*When*—the rain stops!" The King groaned. "Hold fast, brothers! Help any animal you can, we may be able to make it to the grasslands from here. At least some of us have a foothold at last."

CHAPTER EIGHT

M'*Toto Proves He Is Growing Up*

The great elephants held fast to one another and though they drifted down stream they formed a dam over which smaller animals clambered and gained footholds in the steep canyon.

The rains slackened and finally stopped. The late sun peeped out from behind a cloud. Even though the waters still raged the animals ceased to cry and bellow as they waited patiently for the waters to recede.

A fire-scarred antelope darted out of the ravine. "The fires are out! This ravine is steep but passable" he cried before he bounced back up the path switching his singed white tail in a happy signal.

The King raised his great tusks into the air and sent cheering trumpet signals that echoed up and down the canyon. Then he fanned his ears as he listened to the joyous calls that answered him, some from nearby and others faintly from a great distance.

He turned to look down upon his son, M'Toto, whose trunk was gently curled around the tiny dik dik. He touched them softly on the head, then spoke to the Queen and Aunties that stood guard.

"Aunt Koma, you will follow the first line of bulls and carry our little friend, Mydac."

Aunt Koma nodded her big head and lifted the little antelope tenderly. His eyes were wide with fright and he struggled frantically.

"You need help, Mydac, just as we needed help when the fire surrounded us. Please do not be afraid." The King touched the trembling little creature, which quieted him.

"M'Toto will have to follow his mother. Aunt Karia, you stay closely behind him to help him over the steeper grades." The big females nodded their understanding.

The King and his herd slowly led the way up the steep muddy rain-softened ravine. When the slopes were too steep, the elephants scraped the softened earth and rocks into steps and each would stomp down the mounds with their heavy feet so those following could climb with more ease.

After what seemed hours of holding onto his mother's tail with a tight grip while Aunt Karia boosted him from behind, M'Toto at last peered over the top of the small ravine. The sight was very startling. All the earth was black and brown. Even the trees and shrubs were blackened.

M'Toto was helped out of the ravine and stood looking around him open-mouthed. "Mama! What will you eat?" This was the first time M'Toto had thought about food for anyone but himself. As the hundreds of animals that were climbing out of the ravine, passed them he again cried. "Mama, what will they eat?"

The Queen hugged her little son proudly as she answered.

"We will be all right, M'Toto. I don't know where we will find food but the King and his brothers are very wise and they will find something for us all. With the good rains coming down again, the prairies and forest will be such a beautiful green that it will hurt your eyes!"

The King and his brothers stood near the edge of the canyon and touched each elephant as it climbed out. "You must put mud on your burns, brother; it will help to heal them." Another they advised, "Find the big fever trees, we feel sure they have not been destroyed by the fire. Their leaves and gum will help heal your wounds from the boulders and sharp jagged rocks that have cut your skin." Other animals were advised in the care of their wounds as they clambered out of the ravine.

A black-maned lion and his mate moved wearily up the crevice, their golden coats matted with mud and debris. They raised their large yellow-flecked eyes and looked long into the King elephant's, then as though in apology they turned together silently and moved off softly into the twilight.

At that moment, M'Toto remembered Mydac.

"Where is Mydac, my friend?"

The Queen hastily looked around for Aunt Koma before answering but did not see her.

M'Toto misunderstood and shrieked with fear. "Where is my friend, Mydac? Where did you leave him?"

He stopped his noisy accusations abruptly as he heard a faint whistle coming from under a blackened bush. There lay the exhausted little dik dik. The injured hind leg was stretched out straight and he licked it with disinterest.

M'Toto's eyes filled with tears as he touched the thin bloody little leg gently. "I will make it well for you, Mydac! I will nurse you just like the big ones do!"

M'Toto gathered up some mud and awkwardly packed the wounded foot. "I'm sorry you got hurt! So very very sorry. If my mother will place you on my head, I can carry you easily!"

"Forget me, little elephant. Any animal with a bad foot especially at this time of famine—has no chance. Don't worry about me." said Mydac, laying his weary head down.

M'Toto saw that his father, the King, had moved up silently behind him and had heard the dik dik speak. "Please father, we don't leave our friends—do we? I know I can carry him and care for him! PLEASE?"

The King smiled down at his son and nodded gravely as he wiped some of the mud from the little elephant's face. "It would be good for you, son. You have shown that you're ready for this responsibility." Gravely the King lifted Mydac onto M'Toto's back.

The strange undeclared peace that had existed among the many kinds of wild animals during the fire and flood would soon disappear as their fears quieted and their hunger increased. Already the herds of deer, antelope and zebra were spreading quickly over the burned prairies looking for food. But now the fear of their old enemies, the lion, the leopard and the hyena kept them moving very fast.

The King elephant summoned his herd to gather around him. The great grey beasts waited for him to speak, swinging their long trunks, fanning their huge ears, and shifting their ponderous bodies from foot to foot.

"First, I want to thank our little friend the dik dik. He has helped us through a great peril." The King lifted the little antelope from M'Toto's back and carefully raised him high into the air so all the herd could see him.

"Mydac, since none of your kind are here to vote on this, I cannot make you the 'King' of the dik diks but I can make you a PRINCE! And a very royal prince you are. Henceforth you will be known as 'Prince Mydac.' You and all of your kind will be long remembered as the great friends of the elephants."

The elephant herd put their trunks into the air and blew a blast of cheer so loudly that the little antelope trembled with fright.

The King gently placed the dik dik between his large round feet and called to M'Toto. "I also wish to thank my little son, M'Toto, whom most of you already know— very well!" The King's left eyebrow raised as he paused.

"However he has tried very hard to help us all, this time, and for so young an elephant I am very proud of him."

Again the elephant herd cheered and trumpeted "Prince M'Toto! Prince M'Toto!"

M'Toto flipped his tail happily and picked up Mydac from his father's feet and carefully carried him over to the Queen. He could hardly resist squeezing the tiny dik dik to show how proud he was of his brave friend.

The King turned slowly around in the center of the elephants and now he looked at them sadly. "There is not enough food left for all of us—together. We are not in condition to return to our own forests but small groups will be able to forage for enough food to keep them alive until we can meet again. I wish you all well!"

The King, his brothers and the older and wiser elephants held a conference to pick the most suitable locations where the family groups might find food. Though the grasses were burnt and the trees badly singed many still had tender edible twigs. Good roots were still available and now that the fall rains had started and would continue for several months the prairies and forests would soon be green again.

There was much bellowing among the herd as the bulls started to round up their mates and the little ones. None of them wanted to leave his friends but this was the only sensible solution to the famine that otherwise faced them. There were many arguments and a few fights among

92

the bull elephants as someone would try to entice another's female to enlarge his own harem.

The younger males started out together. They were too young for families of their own and too old to be with their mothers any longer. Some of the mothers had two or three younger elephants to look after.

M'Toto nestled against his mother's leg watching with

concern as the elephants fought and divided themselves into groups and moved slowly and sorrowfully away.

"Mama, whom will we go with?" He asked anxiously.

"With the King of course. He is your father. Also his brothers Busia and Gatto as well as Aunt Karia, Aunt Koma, Aunt Hovu and little Tana. And—of course—Mydac?"

She smiled down upon M'Toto, her brave baby elephant as he sighed with relief and rubbed his still furry cheek against his beloved little friend the dik dik.

The gentle rains continued and the ground turned green under their feet as they moved slowly toward their own haven. Mother Nature had once again smiled upon the African land.